Tilly Tiptoes
and the
Grand Surprise

Presented to

Mia Wynne

for Excellent Manners

in the Dinner Hall

from Veira + Nicola

June 2014

Tilly Tiptoes
and the
Grand Surprise

Caroline Plaisted
Illustrated by Hollie Jacobs

Catnip

CATNIP BOOKS
Published by Catnip Publishing Ltd
14 Greville Street
London EC1N 8SB

This edition first published 2011
1 3 5 7 9 10 8 6 4 2

Text © 2011 Caroline Plaisted
Illustrations © 2011 Hollie Jacobs
The moral rights of the author and illustrator have been asserted.

A CIP catalogue record for this book is available from the British Library.

ISBN 978-1-84647-123-0

Printed in India by Replika Press

www.catnippublishing.co.uk

Always remembering Joyce Wells,
who was the Ballet Wardrobe Mistress
at the Royal Opera House

Chapter One

Saturday mornings are the best. And it's not just because I don't have to go to school. Saturday mornings are the best because that's when I go to my special ballet class called Extras.

I love my ballet classes. I love dancing. It makes me feel happy and like I can fly on my toes. I can't remember a time when I didn't dance. My mum and dad say that too. My mum says I was pointing my toes from the minute I was born. My dad says as soon as I could walk, I was running on my tiptoes. That's how I got my nickname.

But hang about, I'm going on about my nickname when you don't even know my real name. OK, my *real* name is Chantilly Tippington. But everyone calls me Tilly Tiptoes – geddit? I'm eight and I've got long brown hair and freckles. I live with my mum, who's called Susanna, and my dad, who's called Nick. Both my parents are dancers. Which is probably why I love dancing too!

Anyway, I was telling you why Saturday mornings are the best. Because of Extras, my dancing class. I started doing Extras a short while ago with my best friend, Rose. Everyone says that Rose and I look totally different. Rose has blonde hair that's shorter than mine, and she's a bit taller than me. In the week, I go with Rose to a ballet class run by our dancing teacher, Miss Nancy. We've been with Miss Nancy since we were four. But just before our eighth birthdays, Miss Nancy suggested that we go to an audition for Extras.

The audition was like a ballet class, but instead of just one teacher, we had loads of people watching us. And I mean *loads*! A whole line of men and women sat at the front of the ballet studio, staring at us. And when we'd finished dancing, we had to do things like stand sideways and bend down and touch our toes for *hours* – soooo boring when you could be dancing instead! But Rose and I didn't mind, because at the end they said we were good enough to join.

The great thing about Extras is that it's at the Grand Theatre. Which happens to be where my mum and dad work. It's run by the teachers of the Grand Ballet and we get to do class in a proper ballet studio with mirrors and everything! Some of the students have gone on to be dancers with the Grand Ballet. So being in Extras makes me feel like I've made my first step to becoming a ballerina!

On Saturday, I went to the theatre with Rose and her mum, Helen. Every time I see the Grand Theatre, I feel excited and get butterflies in my tummy. The place is huge! It's also dead posh and has all this gold paint and shiny glass everywhere. There are these amazing mega-large doors at the front. But for Extras we go round to the side of the theatre, to the Stage Door!

Get that — we actually use the Stage Door. Like *real* dancers! Anyway, on Saturday we went in and Bob, the nice man who sits at a desk just inside the Stage Door, said hello to us. Bob knows everyone at the theatre and he's always very friendly.

'Hello, you two,' he said, grinning. 'Here for your class?'

'Yes!' we smiled.

'You're in the Fonteyn Studio today,' Bob told us. 'Know where that is?'

'Course,' I said. Because of Mum and Dad, I've spent hours — *years* — in the theatre. So I know where most things are.

11

'Jolly good,' Bob laughed. 'Don't forget to point your toes!'

We giggled.

'See you girls later,' said Helen.

And me and Rose set off to our class.

Chapter Two

The corridor was long and dark. All along the walls there were great big notice boards covered in lists. The lists had important stuff on them, like when rehearsals and classes were, and the names of the dancers that were performing in different ballets. Halfway down the corridor, we spotted two people reading a poster.

'Mia!' Rose and I both spoke at the same time.

Remember I said some Extras students

went on to join the Grand Ballet? Well, Mia was in our class last term. Now, she's a proper dancer! She was with a boy I recognised called Gus.

'Hey! How are you doing?' Mia asked.

'Fine thanks,' said Rose. 'What about you? Are you in the new ballet?'

My mum had told us that there was going to be a new ballet. Everyone was really excited about it.

Mia nodded. 'Can you believe it? And Gus is too.'

Gus grinned. 'It'll be my first major ballet since I joined the company.'

'That's great,' I said. 'Let's hope we can come and see you dance!'

'Yes – we'll clap the loudest,' Rose added. 'But we need to hurry now, or we'll be late for class!'

We waved goodbye and sped off down

the corridor, dodging a gigantic wicker basket and a load of violins.

'Hi, Catherine!' I waved at a woman with short curly hair, who was counting the violins and marking them off on a clipboard. Catherine is the orchestra manager.

'Hello, Tilly,' she smiled. 'Are you going to see Jessie later?'

'Of course!' I grinned. I never came to the theatre and didn't visit Jessie.

Jessie is my godmother and she works in the theatre as well. But Jessie isn't a dancer. She's something called a wardrobe mistress, which means she's in charge of all the dancers' costumes. Jessie is lots of fun and I love her to bits.

'Well tell her I need one of her nice cups of tea,' Catherine sighed, scratching her head. 'According to this, I should only have eight violins and I've just counted ten. And some of my music is missing too . . .'

'See you later,' I giggled.

Next stop was the girls' changing room. It was stuffed with other girls who were yanking on leotards and ballet shoes. Rose and I quickly changed, then rushed down to the Fonteyn Studio. Some students were already waiting by the door. You could hear music tinkling from the piano inside.

'What's going on?' Rose asked, trying to take a look.

Veronica, one of the older girls, turned round and shoved Rose out of the way.

'It's a rehearsal, you dweeb,' she snapped. 'And it's just about to finish. So shut up and get out of my way.'

'Oh.' Rose's eyes were watery.

No one speaks to my friends like that, I thought.

'Is there a problem?' I asked Veronica.

'Yes — you two,' Veronica barked. 'So get out of my space.'

Wow — did she have a problem or what?

'Ignore her,' I whispered to Rose, who smiled at me.

We stood and listened to the music.

'Do you recognise it?' I asked Rose.

'Honestly!' Veronica sighed dramatically as she swung round to glare at us. '*Do you recognise it?*' she mimicked. 'Duh! It's only *Giselle*! About one of the most famous ballets *ever*!'

Before I could think of some smart reply, the music stopped. Dancers began to stream out of the studio. Rehearsal over, it was time for our class and Miss Marion, one of the teachers for the Grand Ballet, appeared at the door.

'Good morning, boys and girls,' she smiled. 'Places at the *barre* please – *pronto*!'

I noticed that Vile Veronica made sure she went in first. She took a place right at the front of the *barre* and grinned a sickly sweet smile.

Miss Marion looked around the studio. 'Sorry, I should have said before – can I have boys over there, please?' She pointed

18

to the *barre* nearest the pianist. 'Girls stay here, but taller girls at the back and shorter ones at the front. Same for the boys.'

Ha! Veronica would have to move! I looked at Rose and winked. Being some of the youngest, we were also some of the shortest. So we took our places towards the front of the *barre*. In the huge mirror that took up the whole front wall of the studio, I caught sight of Veronica. She gave us another one of her glares. I had to hand it to her, she was good at those!

'OK.' Miss Marion looked swiftly round the studio. 'And one, and two, and three and *plié* . . .'

Chapter Three

Our ballet class was amazing! As always, we warmed up at the *barre* with our *pliés* and then we did *battement tendu*, where we point our feet and stretch out our legs.

'Keep those feet pointing beautifully!' Miss Marion always calls out. 'And no bent knees, please! Push your feet through the floor.'

Some people find it a bit boring to stand for so long at the *barre*. You see, after we've done those first exercises we have to do *battement frappés,* where we have to strike the ball of our foot on the floor as we push our legs and feet out. Then we do *petite battement* and *rond de jambe* before we are allowed to get to the *grande battement,* where we throw the leg that's away from the *barre* high in air.

That's lots to get through before we're allowed to go into the centre of the studio. But I love it all!

'We're warming up our muscles, boys and girls,' Miss Marion reminds us. 'Doing our *barre* exercises means we are increasing the flexibility of our bodies as well as strengthening the spine. And make sure you don't lean on the *barre!* We're here to improve our balance – after all, there won't be a *barre* in the middle of the stage, will there?'

It's knowing things like that which

makes *barre* work seem more interesting. Knowing that we're improving all those things that will make us faster and stronger on stage. And anyway, even professional dancers like my mum and dad have to do a ballet class every day before they're allowed to rehearse or perform.

At last, Miss Marion moved us into the centre. After starting with our *port de bras* work, which improves our balance with our arms, we finally got to do some floor work including some *sautés*, or jumps, which I absolutely love. The older children in Extras do more complicated things than me and Rose and the other younger ones. We take it in turns to do our sequences of steps and it's really interesting to watch the others. It's a good way to pick up tips!

But the hour-long class was soon over and, after curtseying and bowing our thank yous to Miss Marion and the pianist, we were all back in the changing room, pulling on our jeans.

'My legs feel like jelly,' I declared, thinking about the *adage* work Miss Marion had made us do in the centre.

'I just don't get how some girls can raise their legs so high and not wobble!' Rose said. 'I don't think I'll *ever* be able to.'

'Don't beat yourself up about it,' I said. 'Mum says you just have to practise – keep doing all that *barre* work. You'll crack it eventually. We all will!'

I walked back with Rose to the Stage Door, where her mum was waiting.

'See you on Monday,' I said. 'And thanks for bringing me here, Helen.'

'Bye!' Rose and her mum both waved.

Then it was time for the next best thing of my day – my visit to Jessie.

I went through the bright-red swing doors and found Jessie sitting at the wooden worktable which sits in the middle of the room. It's the biggest table I've ever seen and is surrounded by lots of wooden stools. Sometimes, during the week, all the stools are full of people busy sewing costumes. Today it was just Jessie.

'Tilly!' Jessie called out as I walked in. 'You're just the person I need. I've got a crisis!'

Jessie never has a crisis. Everyone at the Grand Theatre knows that Jessie is the one person who can solve every problem.

'What's up?' I asked.

'I've lost something,' Jessie declared. She looked worried and started picking things up from the table and putting them back down again.

'What?' I asked.

'A sleeve – well, part of one. From Giselle's costume,' Jessie explained.

'How can you lose part of a sleeve?'

'I cut it out and was going to sew it on this morning,' Jessie said. 'Then the phone rang and I had to go and see someone down in the rehearsal rooms. When I came back, it had gone. I'm certain I put it on the table, but I've looked everywhere!'

Ooops! *Giselle* is the new ballet that Mia and Gus are going to be in.

25

'Perhaps you took it with you to rehearsal?' I suggested.

'No – I looked,' Jessie scratched her head. 'I retraced my steps, there and back, and it wasn't anywhere. This is a potential disaster! The first performance is only two weeks away. And I can't get any more of that fabric.'

'Hmmm.'

How could a sleeve – even part of a sleeve – just disappear? And how could the production of *Giselle* go ahead if the main dancer only had part of her costume?

'OK,' I said. 'I'll help you look.'

'Thanks, Tilly.' Jessie came over and gave me a dramatic hug, plonking a kiss on my head as she did. 'You're an angel. A star. My darling, Tilly – find me that sleeve!'

Chapter Four

I looked around the room. The place was stuffed with all sorts of gorgeous goodies. Pots full of sequins, spools of sewing thread in a rainbow of colours, enormous bolts of soft, silky fabric. Yummy stuff that Jessie was going to use to make tutus and other costumes.

How was I going to find a sleeve – a bit of a sleeve – in that lot?

But when Jessie went off to the kitchen to make herself a cup of tea (Jessie is *always*

making cups of tea), I decided to start looking on her worktable.

I picked everything up, turned things over. I even shook things. Nothing.

I looked under the table. Nothing but a whole heap of pins, the odd sequin and shiny bead. I went over to the store cupboard, where Jessie kept things like hooks and eyes, and tape. I wondered if somehow she'd dropped the sleeve in there. But I looked on every shelf and found nothing.

This was so frustrating! I put my hands on my hips and did a slow pirouette glancing round the room. OK, I know a ballerina is meant to 'spot' when she does a spin, so she doesn't wobble, but this was a desperate situation. I had to find that sleeve, so I was prepared to wobble.

I was halfway through my turn when I stopped, looking at a big cabinet in the corner. It was where Jessie kept all the drawings and details of costumes. And it was huge! I bet Jessie had gone over to the cabinet to check something when she was sewing on the sleeve.

I went over and opened the drawers one by one. There were drawings of handsome princes in uniform, wicked witches in scary spiderwebby cloaks, gorgeous princesses in sparkly tutus . . . They were amazing! I was just looking at one of a frog (don't ask me – I've no idea what ballet a frog is in) when I dropped it. It fluttered like a leaf out of my hand and down the side of the cabinet.

I bent down to pick it up. Rats! It had landed right at the back. I stuck my arm up the side of the cabinet and reached as far as I could. It was no good. I turned myself sideways and reached out further.

'Aaargh!' I shrieked.

Something hairy had just brushed against my fingers!

'Tilly? Are you all right? I thought I heard you scream!' Jessie raced into the room, a mug of tea in her hand. She put it down on the worktable.

'Down there!' I said, pointing beneath the cabinet. 'It was down there!'

'What? Have you found the sleeve?' Jessie asked. 'Oh, you marvellous girl!'

'No, not the sleeve,' I spluttered. 'It was hairy! There's something hairy down the side of the cabinet – I felt it!'

Jessie looked at me and then at the cabinet.

'Something hairy,' I repeated. 'That moved!'

'Oh,' Jessie said. 'Like a mouse, maybe? I'd better investigate.'

She took a broom with a long handle from beside another cupboard.

'What are you going to do with that?' I asked.

'I use this to sweep under the cupboards,' Jessie explained. 'It fits in most places because it's flat – see?'

Slowly, she crept towards the cabinet, holding the broom in front of her.

'Here goes!' Jessie shot the broom down the side of the cabinet and flicked it back out again.

'Oh!' we both said.

There on the floor in front of us wasn't a mouse but a slightly dusty piece of fabric. And a drawing of a frog costume. Jessie bent down and picked them up.

'My sleeve!' she exclaimed, shaking off the dust. 'Tilly – you found it!'

'But,' I spluttered. 'I felt something hairy!'

'Hmmm,' Jessie muttered. 'I reckon it must have been the sleeve – you know, with all that dust on it?'

'Well, maybe . . .' I agreed, but I wasn't convinced. The problem was, I didn't know what else it could be.

'Anyone home?'

The door of the ballet wardrobe swung open.

'Mum!' I yelled and raced over to give her a hug.

'Hello, darling,' Mum squeezed me back. As usual, she had her huge bag over her shoulder. It was filled with all sorts of things – ballet shoes, leotards, water bottles, fruit . . . 'Have you been busy?'

'Tilly has saved my day,' Jessie said, and then explained all about finding the missing sleeve.

'Then maybe you can help me,' Mum said. 'I've lost my new leotard. I could have sworn it was in my dressing room yesterday, but I can't find it anywhere! I must have taken it home.'

'I'll look for it there,' I smiled.

'Great,' said Mum. 'Now, Jessie, have you finished with Tilly for today?'

'I think so,' Jessie agreed.

'Good,' said Mum. 'Because we've got some shopping to do!'

Chapter Five

Sundays can be the only day I get to spend time with my mum and dad. They often have a performance on Saturday – sometimes two if there's a matinee. But today there wasn't a matinee or even an evening performance, so I got Mum and Dad to myself for most of the weekend!

After the rehearsal, Dad had to go for a costume fitting so Mum and I went to get some lunch. We went to a café round the corner from the theatre that we go to quite often. The man in the café seems to know all the dancers, and as soon as we arrived he waved at us.

'Hey, Tilly Tiptoes!' he said. 'Are you hungry after all your dancing? How about I make you your favourite toasted cheese and tomato sandwich and bring it over to you with a glass of orange juice?'

'Yes, please!' I grinned and raced to sit at my favourite table by the window.

I like the window seat because, as you eat, you can watch everyone passing by outside.

'What time will Dad be finished?' I asked as I sipped my juice.

'Not too long,' Mum said, 'which gives us just enough time to get you some new ballet shoes. I noticed yours are looking rather tatty – and they're probably getting a bit small too.'

'Yes,' I agreed.

Brilliant! New ballet shoes meant going to my favourite shop, *Dance! Dance!* Even standing outside and looking in the window is a treat because they always have gorgeous things on display. I felt butterflies of excitement as we went inside.

On one side of the shop was all the ballet clothes. There were leotards in every colour – pastel shades, deep tones, neon fabric, glittery and shimmery ones. And then there were the tutus – long ones, short ones, ones attached to leotard tops, and even sparkly ones. I wanted them all! Along with all the ballet socks and tights in colours that mixed and matched with the leotards, there were crossover ballet cardigans and legwarmers too! And I haven't even started to tell you about the skirts and all-in-one dance suits . . .

'Hello, Mrs Tippington!' said Mrs Grace, the lady who owned the shop. 'How can I help you today?'

'We've come to get Tilly some new ballet shoes,' Mum said.

'Certainly,' said Mrs Grace. 'Take a seat and I'll fetch some for you to try on. Would you like satin or leather ones?'

'Leather ones today, please,' Mum replied. 'Pink ones.'

I wriggled in my seat as I took off my shoes. I was still wearing my stripy ballet tights under my jeans. As I waited for Mrs Grace to fetch the shoes, I looked at the samples that were on display. There were leather ones in all colours of the rainbow, and white canvas and satin ones that could be dyed to match a costume. Pointe shoes for dancing on your toes when you are older, as well as tons of different types of shoes for tap, jazz and ballroom. They were all gorgeous!

Mrs Grace reappeared with some pink leather ballet shoes for me to try on. She took them out of the wrapper and I slipped them on my feet and then stood on a special carpet so I didn't get the soles dirty. Mrs Grace pulled the drawstring gently to tighten the shoes to make them a perfect fit. She tied it in a loose bow, tucked that in, and then felt gently around my feet to see if there were any baggy bits anywhere.

I looked down and saw the perfect shoes. They were all shiny and clean and felt soft on my feet. I loved them.

'They look like a good fit,' said Mum.

'They are!' I grinned and Mrs Grace agreed.

We walked along the road with my gorgeous new ballet shoes in a neat little canvas bag. It had a picture of a ballerina on the side and it said *I like to Dance! Dance!* on it. Just as we got to the theatre, Dad came out of the Stage Door.

'Tilly!' he called and came rushing over, gently putting down a great big square parcel he was carrying before scooping me up in his arms and plonking a kiss on my cheek. 'I see you got your new ballet shoes. Come on, then – let's go home. I need your help with something!'

What was Dad talking about? I wondered. And did it have something to do with that parcel?

Chapter Six

All the way home, I kept badgering Dad
to tell me what we were going to do. But
all he would say was, 'You'll find out soon
enough!'

The journey back seemed to take
forever. But at last we got home and Dad
said, 'Let's take this upstairs!'

I raced him to my room and Mum
followed us both, laughing.

Dad put the parcel down. 'Can you help
me open it, Tilly?'

The parcel was wrapped in a thick layer of brown paper, and then it had lots of bubble wrap around it. I still couldn't see what was inside.

'Come on – pull it out!' said Dad.

Eventually, it was unwrapped, and I saw a huge painting, almost as tall as I was.

'Wow!' I gasped. 'It's me!'

STARRING Chantilly Tippington

And it was! Me, in a tutu, on the stage of the Grand Theatre. The painting was just like one of the posters that hung outside the theatre, showing a ballerina in a ballet. And across the bottom, was written: *Starring Chantilly Tippington!*

'It's amazing!' I sighed.

Mum and Dad looked at me and smiled.

'Glad you like it,' Mum said. 'It's lovely, isn't it?'

'The best!' I replied. I couldn't wait to tell Rose about it on Monday at school. 'But who did it?'

'Alfie the scenery painter,' Dad said. 'He used a photo of you and then made up the costume using one of the drawings in Jessie's wardrobe.'

'Mega wow!' I said.

'Right,' Dad said. 'Now let's find a good place to put it!'

We took ages working out exactly which was the best spot to hang the picture. In the end, we put it on the wall opposite the end of my bed. That way, I would be able to see it when I went to bed and when I woke up.

After we'd finished, Mum said that she'd brought home a DVD of her and Dad dancing in a ballet. We snuggled on the sofa watching it and I imagined it was really me in the starring role, just like in the picture upstairs.

Mum sewed the elastic onto my new ballet shoes to keep them on my feet. When they were ready, I slipped them on and twirled around the room. And Dad partnered me – just like he had done with Mum!

Later, Mum and I hunted all around the house looking for her missing leotard.

It wasn't in the laundry, or the bedroom – or anywhere else! She decided to have another look for it in her dressing room.

'You never know,' she said. 'Someone might have picked it up with their practice clothes by mistake.'

And that night, when I went to bed, I gazed at myself in the gorgeous tutu on the picture on the wall, imagining that I was dancing in a real ballet.

Chapter Seven

I told Rose all about the picture on Monday at school.

'It sounds amazing,' she sighed. 'I can't wait to see it!'

But I wasn't able to show it to her that day because Mum and Dad were working. So I went back to Rose's house to have tea and play with her until my parents were finished. I'd brought the DVD of the ballet for us to watch. Rose loved it just as much as I did and we danced together to the music, smiling as we twirled and pointed our toes as hard as we could.

It was late when my parents finally came to collect me. They'd been in a long rehearsal for *Giselle* – after all, it wasn't long before the show started and everyone was working hard to make sure the opening night was perfect in every way.

'You know, I still can't find that leotard,' Mum moaned as we walked the last bit home.

'How weird,' I said, puzzled. How could a leotard completely disappear?

On Tuesdays, Rose and I go to ballet class at Miss Nancy's dancing school.

'What smart new ballet shoes,' she said to me, as we took our places at the *barre*.

'Thank you,' I grinned.

'Now, girls,' Miss Nancy called out. '*Demi pliés* – in first, then second, then third positions, please. Ready? And one, and two, and three, and . . .'

Miss Nancy counted the music in and we began. I remembered to keep my head straight, eyes looking ahead and not down as I bent my knees over my toes into my first *plié*.

'Remember there's an imaginary piece of string being tugged from your head, pulling your body up straight,' Miss Nancy told us.

She says it lots of times during class and it sounds funny, but it does work. It helps you to keep your head held high and your shoulders from rising up. Like a puppet!

As the music continued, and we rose from our bend, we slid out and pointed our outside foot before placing it carefully into second position, ready to follow the flow of the music into our next *plié*.

'Keep those knees over your toes!' Miss Nancy told us. 'No sagging!'

When we'd finished our *pliés* on that side, we rose up onto the balls of our feet and, moving towards the *barre*, we slowly pivoted round to face the other direction. Now Rose was in front of me as I placed my hand lightly on the *barre*, ready to begin the exercises again on the other side.

'You're not in a tug of war with the girls on the other end of the *barre!*' Miss Nancy warned, and we laughed.

It was just like Miss Marion, trying to get us not to grip the *barre*.

'I'm going to come along and lift those hands up in a minute,' Miss Nancy continued, smiling. 'And then we'll see how many of you fall over – stop leaning on that *barre!*'

So with the music starting over again, we began our next lot of *pliés*.

We were learning a dance at Miss Nancy's about finding a bird and rescuing it. Every ballet exam includes a dance that we must do on our own, so we were learning the new steps. We were only halfway through it.

'Try to remember the steps you learned this week,' Miss Nancy said, when it was time for our lesson to end. 'We'll pick up on it again next time. Now, in your lines please, girls, ready for your *reverence*.'

Reverence was the name Miss Nancy gave to our curtsey. We don't just bob a curtsey, we use our arms and perform a *port de bras* as we make deep curtseys to thank our teacher and the pianist. It's practice for when we are real dancers and want to thank our audience for watching us.

Lesson over, Rose and her mum walked me to the theatre, where they dropped me off at the Stage Door.

'Thanks, Helen!' I said, giving her a hug. 'See you tomorrow, Rose!'

Chapter Eight

'Well if it isn't Tilly!' Bob greeted me as I pushed open the Stage Door.

'Hello, Bob!' I grinned.

'Are you here to see Jessie?' Bob asked.

'Of course,' I giggled.

'Excellent. Can you do a very important job for me then?' he said. 'Can you take this envelope to her?'

The envelope was big and fat and quite heavy. I carried it carefully along the corridor to the ballet wardrobe.

'This is for you!' I said, handing Jessie the envelope and giving her a kiss.

'Ooh – I think I know what this is,' Jessie said excitedly. 'I've been waiting for it to arrive. Come on – help me open it!'

I peeled back the tape that was keeping the big envelope sealed. Then I peeped in. There was another bag inside, which I pulled out and placed on Jessie's worktable.

'What's in it?' I asked Jessie.

She put her hand inside and took out a collection of transparent containers. In each one was a selection of different-coloured sequins and beads. They shimmered in the lights of the room.

'Wow!' I gasped.

'Aren't they beautiful?' Jessie sighed.

'What are they for?' I wondered.

'I'm going to use them on the costumes for *Giselle*,' Jessie explained. 'Look at this one.' She held up an especially shiny glass bead that caught the light and made a rainbow of twinkly rays.

'I just love it,' I said.

Jessie smiled. 'Come on,' she said. 'I'll put these away and then you can help me deliver some tights. They're over there.'

Jessie pointed to a wicker trolley that was on wheels. It was a bit like a supermarket trolley only made of basket. Inside the basket were lots of pairs of pink ballet tights, all inside bags. Each bag had the name of a dancer on them.

'Where do we have to take them?' I asked, taking hold of the trolley and starting to push it towards the door.

'Follow me to the dressing rooms!' announced Jessie.

And off we set.

'Anyone there?' asked Jessie, knocking

on the door of the first dressing room.

'Yes!' called a voice. 'Come in!'

It was Mia – you know, the girl I told you about before.

'Hi, Jessie! Hello, Tilly!' Mia smiled.

'We've got some tights for you!' I announced from the doorway. I fished out the bags that had Mia's name on them.

'Oh, thank you,' Mia said.

'And we've got some for the other girls too,' said Jessie, taking out more bags.

Each dressing room, you see, is shared by about four dancers. But the ballerinas in the starring roles have a room all to themselves.

Jessie placed the tights on the dressing tables where the dancers sit to do their hair and make-up.

'OK – on we go!' she said and I followed her along the corridor.

At the next dressing room we found Gus searching frantically in his bag.

'You look like you've lost something,' Jessie said. 'Can we help?'

'It's one of my legwarmers,' Gus sighed. 'I know I had it yesterday! I saw them both here before I went home.'

'Mum's lost her leotard too! I said I'd help her look for it today,' I told him.

'Well,' said Gus. 'If you see my legwarmer in your hunt, let me know – it looks like this red one!'

It took Jessie and me quite a while to deliver all the tights. Finally, we reached Mum's room, which was empty because she was still in her rehearsal.

'Shall we see if we can find that leotard?' Jessie asked.

'I'll look on the floor and you check the dressing table,' I said.

I bent down and started searching amongst the bags of shoes and dance clothes. Then I looked behind the basin – there was nothing. But I stayed on the ground, peeking into every corner. And that's when I spotted a dark purple thing tucked right underneath the radiator.

'Hey!' I said, getting closer. 'Do you think this is it?' I hadn't thought to ask Mum what colour it was. I put my hand underneath and grabbed it. It was certainly a brand-new leotard, even if it was a little dusty.

'Let's hope so,' agreed Jessie.

'Mum must have dropped it,' I said, putting the leotard on her dressing table.

'Well that's one mystery solved,' said Jessie. 'And now we've done our jobs, I reckon it's time for a nice cup of tea!'

Back in the ballet wardrobe, the kettle was just boiled and there was lots of chatter going on. Sitting around Jessie's big worktable were Belinda and Adam, who helped make the costumes, and Mary and Amber, who were dressers. Dressers help dancers to put on their costumes and headdresses for a performance – especially when they have to make a quick costume change between acts.

'Hello,' everyone called as Jessie and I walked in.

Belinda was holding a big piece of paper with writing on it.

'What's that?' Jessie asked. 'What does it say? "Lost"?'

'Yes,' said Belinda. 'We've been asked to put this up on the notice board. Some of the dancers are saying their things have gone missing.'

'That's funny!' I said. 'We've just seen Gus and he's lost a legwarmer!'

'If I didn't know better,' said Jessie, taking a sip of tea, 'I'd say there was a naughty fairy around here hiding things!'

Chapter Nine

Later, at home, I told Mum what Jessie had said about the naughty fairy and all the missing items.

'Well I think the naughty fairy was the one who hid my leotard,' giggled Mum. 'And I'm glad you found it – thank you!'

'But what about all the other things?' I asked.

'Oh they'll turn up,' Mum said. 'People in the theatre are always picking up other people's clothes by mistake. Now, come and help me cook supper. And while we do it, you can tell me all about your ballet class.'

So I did. And then after supper Dad and I played the piano together. Dad's really good at it, but I'm just learning. I like to try playing some of the tunes from the ballets that I listen to. After doing some scales and one of my tunes, Dad suggested we play a duet. He searched through the pile of sheet music on top of the piano.

'Here!' he said, putting some pages on the music stand. 'Let's play this one.'

It was a piece of music about a clock. I looked at my bit and Dad showed me the notes. It sounded just like the ticking of the clock. I had a go. *Tick tock, tick tock* went my fingers. It was easy!

'Come on – let's try it together, Tilly,' said Dad. And he moved closer to the piano to play the bottom notes. 'Ready? Let's go!'

Nodding my head to the beat, I tapped away at the piano keys. It was brilliant! We played the tune about four times, then Dad found us another tune to try, this time a waltz, from *Giselle*! I was enjoying myself so much that I didn't realise that it was time for bed.

'Come on,' said Mum. 'Let's get you upstairs.'

As I changed into my nightdress, I asked Mum some more about *Giselle*.

'Is it a new ballet?'

'Actually, it's a very old ballet,' said Mum, tucking me up in bed and sitting down next to me. 'It was first performed a long time ago, in 1841.'

'Wow!' I said, snuggling up with her. 'What happens in it?'

'It's quite a long story,' Mum said. 'And it's quite sad, and a bit scary…'

'Oh please tell it to me, Mum! Please…?'

'Well,' Mum began, 'it's about a girl, called Giselle of course, who lives in a village, and a boy called Hilarion, who really likes her. One day, a rich man called Albrecht arrives in the village. He sees Giselle and thinks she's beautiful. He starts flirting with her, but he doesn't tell her that he's rich.'

'Why not?'

'Because he wants to see if Giselle likes him for who he is rather than because he has money,' Mum went on. 'But he also has a secret, which I'll tell you about in a minute . . . Anyway, Hilarion gets jealous of Albrecht and tells Giselle to take no notice of him. Giselle's mum also doesn't like Albrecht. She wants Giselle to marry Hilarion and stay in the village.'

'Does Giselle listen to them?' I asked. This was a good story, even it if it was a bit complicated.

'No, she doesn't. But then a group of tourists, including a beautiful princess called Bathilde, arrives in the village. Bathilde and Giselle become friends, but what Giselle doesn't realise is that Bathilde is Albrecht's girlfriend, and that soon they are to marry. And Bathilde doesn't know that Albrecht has been flirting with Giselle!'

'So Albrecht isn't a very nice man then,' I said.

'Well he isn't very honest with the girls, is he?' Mum agreed. 'But Hilarion finds out that Bathilde and Albrecht are engaged, so he tells Giselle. When she sees the two of them together it breaks her heart. She is so sad, she dies . . .'

'That's awful!' I cried. 'What happens next?'

'Giselle is buried in the woods and that night Hilarion goes to visit her grave. But he is scared away by the ghosts of lots of other girls.'

'What girls?' I wanted to know.

'They are girls who have all died of broken hearts and have now decided to haunt any men they come across to get revenge.'

'No way!' I said. 'So what does Hilarion do when he sees them?'

'He runs away – wouldn't you? But then Albrecht arrives. He's feeling terrible about what's happened to Giselle. He's come to her grave to ask her to forgive him. He's most surprised when Giselle's ghost appears. But when Giselle sees that Albrecht is so sad, she forgives him. What she doesn't reckon on, though, is the other girl ghosts coming back. They have been chasing Hilarion around the woods, until he died from fright.'

'Poor Hilarion . . .' I sighed. 'He hasn't done anything wrong.'

'No,' Mum agreed. 'And now the leader of the girls, a ghost called Myrtha, decides that Albrecht must also die, whatever Giselle thinks.'

'Do they kill him too?'

'Well, Giselle did love Albrecht. She decides to dance around him all night to keep him safe from the other ghosts.'

'Does it work?' I asked.

I kind of wanted Albrecht to be punished but I also wanted Giselle to win!

'Eventually, the sun comes up and Albrecht is still alive, grateful to have survived and still be with Giselle.'

'So they live happily ever after?'

'Giselle is exhausted from her dancing and Albrecht realises that Giselle is still only a ghost who can't be brought back from death . . .' Mum said.

'No way! So what does he do?'

'He returns Giselle's body to her grave, where her soul, released now from its earthly ties, rises up to heaven.'

I looked at Mum, my eyes blinking with tears.

'That's so sad,' I sighed.

'I know,' Mum agreed.

'But it must be just the best ballet!'

'It is,' Mum said. 'Really beautiful.'

'I can't wait to come and see it,' I yawned and looked at my picture, imagining I was Giselle in it.

'Time for sleep,' Mum smiled and kissed me on my forehead.

'Night, Mum,' I said.

And straightaway, I fell asleep, still thinking I was Giselle, dancing all through the night.

Chapter Ten

The following day, Dad met me from school and took me to the theatre.

'I've got a rehearsal with Mum this afternoon,' he said. 'So Jessie wondered if you'd like to help her in the ballet wardrobe until we've finished?'

'That would be great,' I said. 'But will I get to see any of the rehearsal? I'd really like to see you dance.'

'I know,' Dad smiled. 'But it's a bit crowded in the rehearsal room today.

Anyway, you're coming to watch on Saturday – you know, after Extras?'

'Result!' I said.

Dad and I got off the bus outside the theatre.

'Afternoon, Tilly,' grinned Bob when he saw us at the Stage Door. 'Just the person I wanted to see.'

'Hello, Bob,' I replied. 'How can I help?'

'I found this in the corridor.' Bob held up a pincushion, which I recognised. It was Jessie's. It was attached to a band that wrapped around her wrist so she could take it with her wherever she went and pin costumes without having to hold the pincushion.

'Jessie must have dropped it,' I said. 'I'll take it to her now!'

'See you later, Tilly!' Dad and Bob said at the same time.

I slipped the pincushion around my wrist, then I walked down the corridor towards the ballet wardrobe. On my way, I passed lots of dancers who were going to and from rehearsals and their dressing rooms. I looked at the posters on the walls and saw that the 'LOST' one was still up on the notice board. It was strange how all those things were missing!

At last, I pushed open the red swing door.

'Hello?' I called, looking around the ballet wardrobe, but it was empty.

'Tilly?'

'Jessie? Where are you?'

'Here!' she said, clambering out from underneath her worktable. 'I've lost something – do you think you could help me find it?'

I giggled. 'Would it be this, by any chance?'

I held out my wrist and waved the pincushion in the air.

'Where did you get that? I've been looking for it all afternoon!'

'Bob found it!' I explained, handing over the pincushion to Jessie.

'Oh, thank heavens,' Jessie sighed. 'I've been dropping pins on the floor all afternoon.' She wrapped the pincushion securely on her own wrist. 'Do you know,' she grinned, 'after all that, I think I need a cup of tea!'

'Of course you do,' I laughed. 'Tell you what – why don't I get the magnet and pick up the pins while you make it?'

'Good idea,' said Jessie.

Jessie had a gigantic magnet, shaped like a horseshoe. It was one of my favourite jobs to walk around waving the magnet across the floor and watching all the pins and needles jump up and stick to it.

When I'd finished scooping up the pins, I sat on a stool at the worktable and started to pull off the pins and needles and place them in a giant box that Jessie kept on the table. There was one section for pins and another for needles – and there were lots and lots of them.

'Thank you, Tilly!' said Jessie, coming back with her tea. Behind her were the dressers, Mary and Amber.

'You'll never guess what the lady in the canteen has just told us!' Mary exclaimed.

'Really,' said Amber. 'You'll never guess!'

'Well go on then – tell us!' said Jessie, sitting down at the worktable.

'You know all those things that have been going missing?' Mary said.

Jessie and I nodded.

'And you know food has been

disappearing from the canteen?' Amber added.

We nodded again.

'Well they only found a carton of milk had been knocked over . . .'

'And?' Jessie wanted to know.

'Only the milk wasn't spilt,' Mary said. 'It was all gone!'

'That's strange,' Jessie agreed.

'Someone's saying there's a ghost in the theatre,' Mary announced.

'That would explain all those things going missing,' Amber pointed out.

I shivered. A ghost! In the theatre?

'Whoever heard of a ghost that drank milk?' Jessie said.

She had a point.

'I don't know,' Jessie went on. 'All these missing things and now we think everything is a mystery. Ghosts! It's just daft if you ask me. Now,' she announced, putting down her mug, 'it's time for us to get those costumes!'

'Which costumes?' I asked, leaping up from my stool. 'Can I help?'

'Help?' said Mary. 'We couldn't do it without you – come on!'

We all left the ballet wardrobe – Jessie, Mary, Amber and me – and walked a short way along the corridor to one of the storerooms. The storerooms are stuffed full of rails of costumes. Every costume and rail is labelled with the names of ballets, characters and dancers, so you can work out who should wear what.

One huge rail had GISELLE written on the label at the end.

'This is what we need,' announced Jessie.

'Oh – what was that?' asked Amber, suddenly pointing to one side of the storeroom. 'Did you just see something shining over there?'

We all looked across to where she was pointing. There was nothing.

'It must have been a sequin,' said Mary. 'You know, catching the light?'

'Maybe . . .' said Amber. 'Oh well. I'll take the front of the rail, Mary – you take the back.'

75

The costume rails, you see, are on wheels. That way, they can be moved easily around the theatre.

'I'll hold the door,' I said.

Jessie went out first, followed by Amber, the costume rail, and then Mary. I was just about to go out when I felt like someone was looking at me. I turned round. Was that something twinkling in the corner – just like Amber had said? I looked again. No. Not a thing.

But I glanced back again as I left the storeroom. There was definitely something strange going on in the Grand Theatre. But I had no idea what it was.

Chapter Eleven

On Thursday, after my ballet class with Rose, Helen dropped me off at the theatre. With all the final preparations for the opening night of *Giselle*, everyone was getting excited. They were also very busy, making sure that everything from the scenery, to the props, to the music, and of course the costumes and dancers, were just right.

When I arrived in the ballet wardrobe, Jessie was busy with Belinda, making a final fitting check on Mia.

'Hey, Mia – you look gorgeous!'

Mia was standing by the worktable in a really beautiful costume. It wasn't a tutu with a stiff, frothy skirt. Instead, it was more like a dress. The skirt was made of soft net that was quite full but hung low and below Mia's knees. The bodice of her costume was made of soft, white fabric and had short puffy sleeves. She was also wearing a sort of waistcoat in a dark-red fabric that laced up in front.

'That's so pretty,' I said, touching the material gently.

'Glad you like it,' said Jessie as she worked, sewing some finishing touches to the costume while Belinda made some adjustments to the bodice at the back.

Just then, Mia's tummy let out a loud rumble.

'Oooh – sorry!' she giggled. 'I'm starving.'

'Didn't you have any lunch?' I asked.

'No,' Mia said. 'I brought in a sandwich, but when I went to the dressing room after this morning's rehearsal, someone else had eaten it.'

'You're joking,' Belinda said.

'Honestly,' giggled Mia. 'All that was left was the foil I wrapped it in.'

'That sounds like the milk that went missing from the canteen,' I said.

'Oh, I heard about that too!' said Mia and Belinda at the same time.

'Sounds like everyone has,' said Jessie. 'Well, I've finished with you now. You'd better get out of this costume and go down to the canteen to find something to eat.'

After Mia left, some more dancers came in for their final fittings and then Jessie,

Belinda and I were on our own in the ballet wardrobe.

I was munching on a biscuit when Mum arrived to collect me.

'You'll never believe it,' Mum announced. 'I've only gone and lost my cardigan. I'm certain I left it on the back of my chair. But now it's not there, I don't know. I seem to be losing everything these days.'

'Something's definitely not right,' said Jessie. 'I've never known a time when so many things have gone missing from the theatre.'

'And do you know,' Mum said. 'I could have sworn there was someone in my dressing room the other day – it was like they were watching me while I did my hair.'

'Do you think there's a ghost in the theatre?' I asked, thinking about the feeling

I had in the storeroom the other day. And about what Amber and Mary had been saying. I shivered at the thought.

'Well I've worked here for years,' said Jessie. 'And I've never heard anyone mention a ghost before. Anyway, I've never heard of a ghost that moves things and eats people's lunch, have you?'

We all started to laugh.

'Perhaps it's a hungry ghost,' I giggled.

'I know *I'm* hungry,' Mum smiled. 'And I'm sure you are too. Come on, darling – time to go home.'

'Thanks, Jessie,' I said, grabbing my coat and school bag. 'See you soon!'

And off we went.

Chapter Twelve

I can't tell you how excited Rose and I were on Saturday morning. As a treat, the whole Extras class had been invited to watch a rehearsal for *Giselle*. Miss Marion had told us that after our class we should change out of our practice clothes and then sit at the front of the rehearsal studio to watch.

As soon as we arrived at the theatre, we could sense there was a lot going on. The place was buzzing with activity. Musicians were racing to their own studio and could be heard tuning up their instruments. In the main dance studio, the whole company was already doing their warm-up class. Jessie waved at me as she raced down the corridor carrying bags of sewing equipment. She was following Adam and Belinda, who were pushing one of the rails of *Giselle* costumes.

'Wow, it's busy today,' said Rose as we stood to one side. We were making space for a man who was pushing an enormous basket on wheels.

'What do you think was in there?' wondered Rose.

'A bunch of props?' I suggested. 'I think I've seen one of those baskets backstage.'

'Oh it's so exciting, isn't it?' sighed Rose as we continued down the corridor.

When we got to the changing room,

it was no surprise that Veronica was there already. She was talking to a group of older girls, who were listening in awe to every word she said.

'Of course I've seen *Giselle* before,' Veronica announced. 'It's a really sad story. I'd love to be Giselle myself one day.'

I looked at Rose and winked. Whatever ballet was on at the Grand Theatre, Veronica had always seen it before. She tried to make out she was an expert. Rose smiled back at me as we slipped into our leotards and ballet shoes.

'So when did you see *Giselle*?' I asked Veronica, when I was changed.

Veronica turned and looked down at me. Which isn't that surprising because she's about a foot taller than I am.

'I'm sorry,' she sneered. 'Did you say something?'

'Yes,' I smiled. 'I just heard you saying you'd seen *Giselle* before. I was wondering when you'd seen it?'

'And what's that got to do with you?' Veronica snapped.

'I was just asking,' I said. 'My mum told me they've haven't done *Giselle* here for ages, so I was just wondering what ballet company you'd seen doing it?'

'I . . . I . . .' Veronica stuttered and her cheeks started to go red. Anyone would think I'd caught her fibbing about seeing the ballet. 'I saw it on DVD,' she finally managed to say.

'Cool!' Rose said. 'Could I borrow it?'

'No, you can't!' spat Veronica. 'Now get out of my way. The rest of us want to be on time for class.'

And with that, Veronica pushed past us and stalked off to the studio.

All through class, I imagined I was on stage, dancing as Giselle. When I did my *jétés*, I thought of Giselle dancing at the party after Bathilde and the tourists have arrived. Then, when I did my *glissades*, *sautés* and *grand jétés*, I imagined I was Giselle dancing to save Albrecht's life.

Actually, I think a lot of us were thinking the same thing because you could feel the excitement of everyone in the room. And even though I was loving the class, I couldn't wait for it to end so that we could get to the rehearsal! Vile Veronica seemed to be in a hurry too, because Miss Marion kept on telling her to slow down.

After the fourth time, Miss Marion clapped her hands and said, 'No, no, no!'

The pianist stopped playing and we all stopped dancing.

'Veronica, listen to the beat – one, two, three, one, two, three! Slow it down – you're not running to catch a bus!'

Veronica's face flushed red as everyone in class turned to look at her.

'Let's start again, please. And one, and two, and . . .'

Off we danced again. But Veronica had

obviously got her knickers in a twist about the steps because she set off on the wrong foot, dancing in the wrong direction! Then – BUMP – she crashed into the other girls in her line.

Miss Marion clapped her hands and the music stopped, again!

Now Veronica's face was so red it wouldn't have been surprising if steam had come out of her ears.

'Let's mark it out, everyone,' Miss Marion said, coming to stand next to Veronica. She took hold of her hand. 'Like this, dancers!'

Miss Marion marked the steps by placing her feet and arms in the right positions but without any springs or big movements.

'Have we all got that?'

'Absolutely,' replied Veronica.

But she didn't seem that convinced. Rose looked at me, her eyes boggling a bit. We both knew that Veronica loved attention. But she wouldn't be enjoying this one bit.

'Into position and we'll take it from the top please!' Miss Marion said, waving her arms to move us back. 'Veronica's line go last, please, to give yourselves a chance to learn it properly!'

Veronica looked as if she was going to cry!

The music started again and my line danced first. After watching three other lines of dancers go through the steps, it was Veronica's line's turn. And I can't tell you how pleased she was to get to the end on time with the music and in the right sequence of steps.

'Now,' said Miss Marion, when they'd finished. She looked at the studio clock. 'We'd better stop there or we'll miss too much of the rehearsal. *Reverence* please.'

Chapter Thirteen

As the last tinkling of the piano faded away, Miss Marion clapped her hands for our attention one more time.

'Hurry up, everyone,' she said. 'Change out of your practice clothes so you don't get cold. I'll be waiting outside in five minutes to take you into the rehearsal.'

Rose and I raced back to the changing room with the others. We didn't chat like we normally did. Instead, we got dressed quickly and whizzed back outside to where

Miss Marion was waiting. She walked us along to the main studio, where we could hear the pianist playing.

Miss Marion peered through the small window at the top of the door.

'We'll just wait for a break in the dancing before we go in,' she said.

And then, when the break came, I don't know how she managed to do it, but Vile Veronica managed to shove her way into the studio first!

Miss Marion told us to sit in a single row, pressed up against the mirrors at the front of the dance studio. If you can imagine it, it was like we were sitting in the audience of the theatre and the rest of the dance studio was the stage. And Veronica managed to get herself slap bang in the middle of the row. So she could see absolutely everything. I sat with Rose at the end.

Dad winked at me from across the studio. Mum, though, was busy talking to the man who was taking the rehearsal. He was giving her tips about something.

Then, after a few minutes, the man clapped his hands together and the studio fell completely silent. Everyone, me and Rose included, looked at the man expectantly.

'OK, ladies and gentlemen. Let's start from the top.'

My mum and dad, along with the other dancers, moved into their positions. In the corner of the room, the pianist played a few introductory chords and then the dancing began again.

Along with Rose and the other Extras, I watched entranced by the magic the dancers feet were making as they moved across the studio. In seconds, I realised that the scene we were watching was from the beginning of the ballet. My mum was dancing Giselle and I realised that Dad was Hilarion. Another man was dancing with them – Albrecht. This must be the moment when Giselle meets Albrecht for the first time. And Hilarion was getting very cross and jealous indeed.

I got lost in the music and movement and completely forgot that I was in a rehearsal studio in the Grand Theatre. As far as I was concerned, I was in a small village, watching Giselle flirting with Albrecht. It was brilliant! I couldn't believe it when Miss Marion told us that an hour had gone and it was time to leave.

'I wish we could have seen more,' Veronica said to Tomas, the boy who had been sitting next to her, as we filed out of the studio. 'Nick Tippington is so handsome!'

Rose nudged me with her elbow, but we kept quiet, eager to hear what else Veronica was going to say.

'You know he's married to Susanna Tippington, the ballerina who was dancing the lead part?' she carried on.

Tomas looked at her strangely. 'Well, yeah,' he said. 'They're Tilly's parents.'

Veronica glared at Tomas, as if she hadn't understood what he'd just said.

'No,' she hissed. 'I don't think you heard me. I was talking about Nick and Susanna Tippington – not dancers in the *corps de ballet*.'

Huh! Who did Veronica think she was? And what was wrong with the *corps de ballet* anyway?

'Um,' said Tomas. 'Yes, them. I think you'll find they *are* Tilly's parents.'

Veronica swung round to give me a puzzled look as we headed out of the studio. I stopped in front of her and grinned.

'I'm glad you thought my mum and dad were good,' I said. 'I thought they were terrific!'

And Veronica's jaw dropped wide open.

Ha! That got her.

Chapter Fourteen

'That was proper amazing!' Rose and I said to Jessie afterwards.

'So you think it's going to be good then,' she asked, as we waited in the ballet wardrobe for Rose's mum to collect us.

'Just a bit!' said Rose. 'I can't imagine how it will be with the costumes and scenery and everything.'

'And just think how amazing the music will sound with the whole orchestra playing,' I said.

'There's less than a week to go till the first performance,' said Jessie. 'Are you looking forward to Friday?'

Rose and I looked at each other in surprise.

'You're coming to the opening night, aren't you?'

'Are we?' we both exclaimed.

'Well, I think so . . .' said Jessie. 'But I might have got it wrong . . .'

'I hope not!' I sighed.

I really, really, wanted to see *Giselle*. And if I could go to the opening night with Rose, it would be the best thing ever. I absolutely, definitely, hoped that Jessie hadn't got it wrong!

I couldn't wait to ask Mum and Dad, but they were working late that night, so I was fast asleep when they got home. But over breakfast, as my still-sleepy parents sipped their hot drinks, I pounced.

'Now why on earth would you want to see *Giselle*?' Dad said, peering up from his cup of tea.

'What do you mean?' I gasped. Surely Dad realised how desperate I was to see the ballet in all its splendour?

Mum giggled and turned to Dad. 'Honestly, Nick! You're such a tease.'

I looked from Mum to Dad, who began to grin.

'How about Friday?' he said. 'Do you think you're free then?'

I gasped. 'The opening night? Of course I am! Yes, yes, yes!'

Mum and Dad laughed as I leapt up from my cereal bowl and gave them both a big hug.

'And can Rose come too?' I wondered.

Mum and Dad looked at each other and then at me.

'Well, it was going to be a surprise . . .' Mum said. 'But yes! We've got three tickets – Helen is going to take you and Rose.'

'Brilliant!' I declared, jumping up and down. 'Thank you, thank you, thank you!'

But I didn't have to wait until Friday to see a bit more of *Giselle*. Because on Tuesday, after school, I went to the theatre to wait for Mum and Dad and there was a dress rehearsal going on. A dress rehearsal is where all the dancers put on the costumes they'll be wearing in the performance. And it happens onstage, with the orchestra and conductor in the orchestra pit and everything. Only it's completely different from a real performance because as well as the dancers, you can also see other people walking around onstage, like Jessie, going round adjusting costumes.

The other thing that's different is that the performance stops and starts as the director and the conductor ask questions and check that things are right. So the orchestra might adjust the timing of the music, or the director might ask a dancer to change their position. Sometimes, the people who organise the lighting and scenery get asked to make changes too.

When I arrived, I slipped into a seat in the orchestra stalls and sat silently, watching and listening. I even spotted Miss Marion telling some of the dancers to point their feet more and to hold their heads in a different way, just like when she takes an Extras class!

I was loving every minute of it. The costumes were just gorgeous. And I saw Mia in the dress that I'd seen Jessie and Belinda fitting on her. Mum, as Giselle, wore a similar costume. Only the bodice on her dress was more colourful and fancy. I guessed it was to make her stand out from the other girls. And it worked.

I don't know how long I sat and watched. I was lost in the ballet and didn't really want it to stop. I was listening to the music – the crescendo of the violins and the call of the trumpets when, quite suddenly, I realised I could hear another noise rising above everything.

I turned to look behind me. There was a women in the audience, and she was screaming at the top of her voice!

Chapter Fifteen

'Someone hairy just touched me!' she yelled.

The orchestra stopped playing and all the dancers stood still. Everyone in the theatre turned and looked at the woman, who continued to scream.

'There's no one there! But they touched me! And spoke to me!'

What *was* she talking about? How could someone touch her and talk to her if they weren't there?

The director leapt off the stage and raced over to the woman. He looked really cross and like he was going to tell her off for interrupting the rehearsal. At the same time, the theatre manager appeared.

'Is everything all right, madam?' he asked. 'Are you hurt?'

I know the woman was making a fuss. And I know that she'd interrupted the rehearsal and now everyone was standing around, tapping their feet and looking cross. But the woman looked really frightened and upset. In fact, she looked quite freaked out. She leapt up from her seat and started to gasp for air.

'It was staring at me. And then it touched me,' she spluttered, her eyes wide. 'And then it made a noise! But when I turned round, there was nothing there!'

The theatre manager tried to calm her

down and someone brought her a glass of water. People were rushing around. They were looking for the person — or was it *thing*? — that had touched her. But there was nothing there.

Then the lady started to look round frantically. Like she was searching for something else.

'My scarf! It's gone! It was round my neck! I'm sure it was!'

There was more hunting around. But the scarf couldn't be found. It wasn't on the floor, or on any of the seats. Then someone else in the audience started saying that they'd felt something hairy go past their legs. Everyone was panicking and there was lots of noise as others started shrieking too.

By now, some of the dancers and stage technicians had come off the stage and were gathering round. People were talking to each other about what could have scared the lady and the other people in the audience.

'Do you think there really is a ghost in the theatre?' asked Sophie, one of the dancers.

'Well it would explain all the weird things that have been happening around here,' said another dancer.

But the lady said something about the 'ghost' being hairy. Which made me think about the hairy thing that I had felt brushing against my arm down the side of Jessie's cupboard.

Are there such things as hairy ghosts?

Mum and Dad spoke about it at supper that night.

'What do you think about this ghost?' I asked. 'Can it be true?'

'I doubt it,' said Dad. 'I've never seen anything spooky in the Grand Theatre and I've been working there for a long time now. Although . . .'

'What?' I wanted to know.

'Well the other day, I thought I heard a noise in my dressing room. And the door slammed shut on its own. But I didn't see anything. The noise must have been coming from the pipes.'

So even Dad thought there might, just, be something in this ghost idea! I shivered in my seat. I love going to the Grand Theatre. But I'm not sure I want to be there if there's a ghost about!

Chapter Sixteen

I couldn't wait to tell Rose all about it.

'How freaky!' she said. 'What if a ghost comes into Extras one Saturday? Do you think ghosts can dance?'

'Perhaps it's the ghost of a dancer!' I said.

'Yes! Someone who died young and couldn't fulfil her chance of becoming a ballerina!' Rose's eyes grew big at the thought.

'How creepy is that?' I shrieked. 'Maybe

she's already been doing class with us and we haven't even noticed! I'm going to have to ask Jessie!'

I spoke to her about it at after school. But Jessie said she'd never heard stories about any dancers who'd died young.

'I haven't even heard one about a dancer who got injured and had to end their career early,' she said, sipping her tea. 'In fact I think this whole ghost idea is a bit silly. And we certainly don't have time for it to interrupt our preparations for the opening night. If we keep having to stop rehearsals, we'll never be ready on time!'

'But what was it that spooked that lady yesterday?' I demanded. 'She said it was hairy! And I felt that hairy thing down the side of your cupboard, didn't I?'

'You mean the hairy thing that turned

out to be Giselle's sleeve covered in dust and fluff from the floor?' Jessie grinned.

'Hmmm – I see what you mean,' I giggled.

'There will be a perfectly ordinary explanation for everything,' Jessie assured me. 'And then we'll all wonder what we got ourselves so worked up about! Now, I've got some jobs to do – fancy giving me a hand?'

'You bet,' I said and jumped up from my stool.

First, we delivered some headdresses and shoes to various dressing rooms. Then Jessie asked me if I could take a pile of forms to the director's office.

Serena is the director's assistant and I found her in her office near to where Bob sits by the Stage Door.

'Oh thanks, Tilly,' Serena said when I

gave her the forms. 'I was waiting for these. Are you going back to Jessie now?'

I nodded.

'Then could you give her this, please? It'll save me a job.' Serena handed me an envelope.

As I went down the corridor, I listened to the music that was playing over the tannoy system. The tannoy is a way of sending messages to people throughout the back of the theatre, but you can't hear it anywhere the audience goes.

During a performance, the music of the orchestra is played over the tannoy. That way, the dancers in their dressing rooms and the people in the ballet wardrobe can tell what's happening onstage. And the stage manager also uses it to give directions to everyone, telling them how long it will be before curtain up and when certain dancers should be in the wings or on stage.

I walked along, singing to the music of *Giselle*. But when I got back to the ballet wardrobe, Jessie wasn't there. Nor was anyone else. So I took out Jessie's magnet to help pick up some pins and needles that had got spilt.

I bent down and got under the worktable. There were loads there. I waved the magnet around and there was a gentle tinkling noise as all the pins zoomed up from the floor. Then I started working my way across the room.

I moved towards the big cupboard, where Jessie keeps all the special material and stuff. And found more pins! *Clink, clink* they went as they were sucked up onto the magnet.

And that's when I felt it. The feeling that I was being watched. Again.

I looked around. The wardrobe was still empty except for me. I shivered.

And that's when I heard it. A rustling noise. It was coming from the side of the cupboard!

I leant across and peered down. And two beady eyes stared back at me.

I screamed!

Chapter Seventeen

I screamed some more!

'What is it?' said Jessie, rushing into the room. 'Are you hurt?'

'Eyes! There are eyes down the side of the cupboard! It's the ghost!' I shrieked.

'Ghost? Eyes?' Jessie said. 'Let me take a look . . .'

Jessie peered down the side of the cupboard, and as she did, Belinda and Adam also raced into the room.

'We heard screaming,' said Adam.

'Is everything all right?'

'It's the ghost!' I said, pointing to Jessie and the cupboard. 'I saw it! Really I did! It has two beady eyes!'

'Well I never!' said Jessie, standing up.

'Did you see the ghost?' I asked, my eyes wide with fear. But at least I wasn't on my own any more!

'I didn't see a ghost,' said Jessie. 'But I did see something . . . Adam! Belinda! I need your help to move this cupboard.'

'Don't let it escape!' I yelped.

'We won't,' said Jessie.

I watched from the other side of the worktable as the three of them pushed the cupboard to one side. It took them a while and then I heard Belinda say, 'Well, would you look at that!'

'Oh my goodness!' said Adam.

'What is it?' I wanted to know, peering

across the table from behind my fingers. I was terrified I might see a hairy beast.

But what I actually saw was the sweetest little white cat!

The cat was staring at us. She looked very thin and a bit scared.

'She's made a hiding place behind the cupboard,' Jessie said. 'And look what we have here!'

'Careful – don't crowd her,' Adam said quietly. 'She might run away.'

'I don't think there's any chance of that,' said Belinda. 'Look!'

And we looked down at the cat's tummy . . . where four gorgeous little kittens were snuggled up, asleep.

'Oh!' we all sighed. They were so cute. And they were surrounded by a nest of clothing. There was Gus's missing legwarmer, a cardigan or two, and some other bits and pieces . . . including the scarf belonging to the lady from the dress rehearsal.

'I think we've found our ghost,' said Jessie.

'And who's been looking after our lost property,' Adam added.

'She must have taken the milk from the canteen,' I pointed out.

'And those bits of food,' added Belinda.

'Well at least we've solved our mystery,' said Jessie. 'But how on earth did she get here? And what, I wonder, are we going to do with her?'

Adam and Belinda raced down to the canteen and found the cat some food and water. She tucked into it immediately, while her kittens stayed huddled together, asleep. I sat a little distance away, watching them. I was desperate to pick one up, but Jessie said if we interfered too much, the cat might get worried and take the kittens off to another hiding place. When the cat finished eating though, she nested back with her kittens, who made tiny mewing noises as they suckled. The cat began to purr gently and almost looked as if she had a smile on her face.

'We'd better make up a proper bed for

them,' said Jessie. 'How about we use one of our smaller baskets?'

Jessie and Belinda lined the basket with some scraps of fabric and a couple of towels and placed it near to the cat's chosen spot by the side of the cupboard.

'It needs to be a bit sheltered,' said Jessie. 'She'll feel happier and safer for her kittens that way.'

'She's taking a look at it,' I said as we watched the cat sniff the new bed.

'If we put some of her existing bedding in the basket,' suggested Adam, 'she might feel more at home . . .'

After rubbing herself around the new basket, as if she was marking her scent on it, the cat rolled onto her back and then looked at us, as if trying to work out if she could trust us.

She must have decided she could,

because then she stood up and, one by one, lifted her kittens into the basket before snuggling up with them again.

'Who do you think she belongs to?' I asked Jessie.

'No idea,' Jessie replied. 'But we'd better see if we can find her owner. They'll be worried sick.'

'I know, I'll make a poster!' I suggested.

And I spent the rest of the afternoon doing just that.

News about the cat spread round the theatre. Dancers kept coming into the ballet wardrobe to take a peek into the basket, and lots of them recognised their missing items of clothing.

One of the last visitors that afternoon was Catherine, the orchestra manager.

She looked at the poster that I was putting the finishing touches to.

'That's a great idea,' she said. 'Shall I photocopy it for you? Then we can ask all the local shops to put it up.'

'Oh yes,' I smiled. 'Thank you!'

So that night, after rehearsal, Mum, Dad and I visited as many shops as we could and they all promised to put up the poster. It wouldn't be long before the cat, and her kittens, would all be going home, I thought happily.

Chapter Eighteen

Surprisingly, no one came to the theatre the following day to claim the cute little cat. So she and her kittens stayed in the ballet wardrobe and seemed very happy there whilst the final frantic preparations were made for *Giselle*.

After getting over her initial shyness, the cat seemed to love all the attention and began to make friends with everyone, purring as they stroked her head. When she was curled up with her kittens in their basket, I think she was even listening to the music over the tannoy. Her ears twitched in time with the beat!

The next day was Friday, and opening night. Rose and I were so excited about it we could hardly concentrate at school.

Helen got us to the theatre early so we could pop into the ballet wardrobe before the show started. I wanted to introduce them to the cats.

'Isn't she gorgeous,' said Rose, petting the cat who was lying on her side in her basket, feeding her kittens. 'Her fur is like snow.'

'I know,' I grinned, stroking her head. 'It's just like Giselle's dress at the end of the ballet – you wait till you see it. It's gorgeous too.'

But suddenly we were interrupted by the voice of the stage manager on the tannoy.

'Twenty minutes to curtain up,' he warned. 'Twenty minutes to curtain up.'

We all gasped and Jessie, who was about to whiz off to make a last-minute adjustment to someone's costume said, 'Looks like you'd better go and take your seats. Have a great time!'

'Thanks, Jessie,' said Helen. 'Come on, girls!'

Just minutes later, Helen, Rose and I were sitting in the stalls. There was a buzz of excitement from the audience as we all eagerly awaited curtain up.

Sitting forward in my seat, I could feel butterflies in my tummy. I wondered how Mum and Dad and all the other dancers were feeling as they stood backstage, doing a few more *pliés*, waiting to perform.

'Isn't this fantastic?' said Rose as we heard the musicians tuning up.

'It's starting,' I whispered, grabbing Rose's hand as the lights began to go dark and the orchestra went completely silent.

The audience fell silent too as the conductor walked into the orchestra pit to stand on his podium and raised his baton. With the first bars of music rising from the musicians, the opening performance of the Grand Ballet's production of *Giselle* had begun!

The curtain went up on the scene of the village where Giselle lived. There was lots going on as we realised that the villagers were preparing for the harvest. Dad looked fantastic as Hilarion and Mum looked gorgeous in her white dress and waistcoat – it wasn't really surprising that Albrecht started flirting with her.

Then, when the harvest had been brought in, Giselle was made Queen of the Harvest and Rose and I were caught up in the light-as-air steps that Mum was making. I wished I could be that good on my toes.

But boy was it sad when Hilarion told Giselle about Albrecht having a girlfriend. Giselle went bonkers! She blew a hunting horn to get everyone's attention and then ran her fingers through her hair she was so mad. Wow! The curtain fell as the heartbroken Giselle died . . .

We sat in silence for a moment and then Rose and I both spoke at the same time: 'That was so sad!'

'I love all the costumes,' declared Rose. 'And the scenery. It's totally amazing!'

'Your mum and dad are fantastic, Tilly,' said Helen. 'You must be so proud!'

I nodded. I was so proud, I thought I might burst!

Helen's mum bought us an ice cream and after we'd eaten it, Rose and I went to have a peep into the orchestra pit. We could see the musical scores sitting on the music stands and all the bits and pieces that the musicians took into the pit with them. But before long, we heard the bell going outside in the auditorium.

'The second act is about to start!' gasped Rose.

'Quick – let's get back to our seats!' I said.

The curtain rose slowly and poor Hilarion was sitting weeping at Giselle's woodland grave. Pretty soon, he was surrounded by the ghosts of all the broken-hearted girls. They may have been ghosts but their tutus, which had long skirts, were gossamer and gorgeous. I felt really sorry for Hilarion, who looked petrified of the ghosts as they swarmed on him and scared him away. Then Albrecht appeared. It was difficult to remember that he'd been the cause of all the trouble because he looked so sad. I could see why Giselle felt sorry for him!

When the scary Myrtha, the Queen of the ghostly girls, declared that Hilarion was to die I wanted to call out 'no!' and save Dad. He lay there, slumped on the stage as Myrtha turned on Albrecht. Giselle then started to dance with Albrecht, protecting him from the ghosts of that awful night. Finally, when dawn broke and Albrecht returned Giselle's body to her grave, I could feel a tear running down my cheek. I wiped it away and then, as the curtain fell, rose up from my seat along with everyone else in the theatre and clapped and clapped until my hands hurt!

Flowers were thrown on the stage, and Mum was given a fabulous bouquet too. The applause went on for absolutely ages. When it eventually stopped, we gathered

our coats and slowly made our way out
of the theatre.

'I want to see it again!' said Rose.
'It was incredible.'

'Wasn't it wonderful?' I sighed, linking
my hand in Rose's.

And we skipped and galloped our way
to the Stage Door.

Chapter Nineteen

'That was A-MAZING!' we screamed, when my mum and dad finally appeared, tired but with faces flushed from the excitement of the evening.

'You liked it then?' said Dad, grinning.

'You bet!' I said.

We talked about it all the way home and Mum and Dad said how much they'd loved being part of the performance.

The next morning Rose and I were still humming the tune and dancing to it when we arrived at Extras.

'What are you two so excited about?' Veronica wanted to know as we waited for our class to begin.

'We were just talking about seeing *Giselle* last night,' I explained.

'You mean you've been? *Already?*' Veronica glowered.

We nodded.

'That's so not fair!' said Veronica. 'I'm going tonight . . . I . . . I . . .'

'You'll love it,' said Rose.

'But how did you get tickets for opening night? My mum said they sold out immediately. *I* wanted to go last night! I've been at Extras longer than you two – *I* should have been there!'

'Mum and Dad got them,' I explained.

'There were in the leading roles, after all,' said Rose.

'Huh! That's so not fair!' said Veronica, and turned on her heel and stormed into the studio to take a place at the front of the *barre*.

Rose and I looked at each other and laughed.

'She's sure got a problem!' giggled Rose.

We entered the studio along with everyone else and went to find our places. Miss Marion was already inside, talking to the pianist. When she'd finished, she turned to us.

'Now what have I told you before?' she sighed. 'Tallest girls at the back, please! Veronica – can you move to the other end?'

'But . . .' Veronica spat. 'I'm never at the front.' She looked really cross.

'You will be when we turn around,'

said Miss Marion. 'Come on, Veronica –
move along now.'

'Huh!' Veronica grumbled.

But you couldn't feel sorry for her.

After class, I went to see Jessie. And of course
the cat and kittens, who were snuggled
against their mother, feeding.

'Did you enjoy last night?' Jessie asked.

'Did I just!' I exclaimed and then I told
Jessie all about what I'd seen from the front
of the theatre, and how the atmosphere
had been electric.

We talked for ages, and Jessie told me
about the excitement that had happened
backstage and in the wings.

'It was an exhausting evening,' she said.
'We were all so determined to get it right,
we couldn't relax until the curtain fell.'

Just then, the beautiful white cat jumped onto Jessie's worktable. Her kittens, now full of milk, were sleeping soundly in their basket.

'Well, hello,' I said, tickling her under her chin as she purred. 'Has anyone called the theatre about her today?'

'No,' Jessie shook her head. 'Isn't it strange? A beautiful cat like her. But I'm sure the owners will turn up soon. And then we'll know what she's called!'

As the cat purred contentedly and nuzzled at my hand, Jessie took something from one of her cupboards. She placed a tin on the table that had a picture of a ballerina on it.

'That looks like Giselle!' I said.

'It's pretty, isn't it?' agreed Jessie. 'And it's got rather nice biscuits inside! Here – have one.'

The cat continued to purr as she explored the worktable while we munched on our biscuits.

'She seems to like it here,' I said to Jessie.

'Mmm,' sighed Jessie, stroking the cat's back. 'And I've rather enjoyed having her and the kittens with me. I'm going to miss them when she goes home . . .'

Chapter Twenty

The following week, when I went to see Jessie again, the biscuits had all been eaten. But the cat and her kittens were still in the ballet wardrobe.

The kittens were much bigger than when we'd first found them – and much noisier. They were so funny as they played and wrestled with each other. One of them was especially pretty with little black toes.

'Oh I could watch them for ages,' I said. 'They're so cute!'

'I know,' agreed Jessie. 'I waste lots of time doing that.'

Just then, the cat stood up from the basket. She jumped up onto the worktable and, after inspecting everything including me, curled up on Jessie's lap.

'I've got a present for you,' said Jessie.

She pushed the Giselle biscuit tin towards me. 'I thought you'd like to have this as a keepsake box.'

I took the beautiful tin from her. There was a rattling noise inside it.

'Thanks,' I said. 'But what's that noise?'

I opened the tin and saw some shiny, twinkling beads and sequins.

'These are the same as the ones on Giselle's costume!' I exclaimed.

'That's right,' said Jessie. 'After all your help in preparing for the ballet, I thought you might like them as a memento.'

'Oh, thank you,' I exclaimed, holding the beautiful beads in my hands. 'I'm going to use this as my ballet box. And keep all my special ballet souvenirs in it.'

Two weeks later, Jessie still had her cattery. The cat and her kittens were all looking plump and healthy. They were also full of mischief, especially the one with the little black toes.

'I've spoken to the theatre manager,' Jessie announced as she sipped her tea, the cat curled up on her lap. 'As no one's claimed the cat, he's decided that she can stay and live with us. She's going to become the Grand Theatre cat!'

'That's great news,' I said. 'But what about her kittens?'

'We'll have to find homes for them,'

Jessie explained. 'But lots of people in the theatre have said they'd love to take one.'

'Lucky them,' I said, stroking the cat.

'We'll need to think of a name for her,' Jessie said. 'Any ideas?'

I thought for a moment and, as I stroked her gorgeous white fur, it came to me.

'Easy,' I declared. 'Let's call her Giselle! She's white. She's beautiful. And we all thought she was a ghost!'

When Mum came to collect me later that afternoon, I was playing with the kittens.

'Jessie was telling me that the kittens will need homes,' said Mum as she crouched on the floor to play with them as well.

'This one is so cute,' I said, showing her my favourite kitten. Her black toes make it look as if she's wearing pointe shoes.

I snuggled the kitten and she kissed my nose.

'Oh, she is gorgeous, isn't she?' said Mum.

I stroked the black-footed kitten, hoping that she'd find a lovely home. Although not too soon because I loved cuddling her and I'd miss her when she left.

'Well I know someone who'd be able to give that kitten lots of love,' Mum said to Jessie.

'Who?' I asked.

Mum smiled. 'How about you, Tilly?'

Me? Mum was going to let *me* take one of the kittens home? I looked at Mum, and the little kitten did a little skip on my lap. We all laughed.

'Yes, please!' I said.

'What will you call her?' Jessie asked, stroking the kitten's head.

'Myrtha,' I announced. 'Like the Queen of the ghost dancers in *Giselle*.'

'Great idea,' said Jessie.

'Yes, perfect,' Mum nodded.

'Miaowwww!' Giselle and Myrtha agreed.

Look out for more adventures starring
Tilly Tiptoes and all her friends
at the Grand Ballet

Tilly Tiptoes
and the
Gala Show

The Grand Ballet are getting ready for the new
production of Cinderella, but Tilly has other things
on her mind. Her ballet exam is looming, and she
just can't remember the steps, and Vile Veronica is
being as nasty as ever. But when one of the dancers
falls ill, will this mean curtains for opening night,
or can Mia step in and save the day?